DOVER
CHILDREN'S THRIFT CLASSICS

Favorite Poems of Childhood

EDITED BY PHILIP SMITH

Illustrated by Harriet Golden

DOVER PUBLICATIONS, INC.
New York

DOVER CHILDREN'S THRIFT CLASSICS
EDITOR: PHILIP SMITH

Copyright © 1992 by Dover Publications, Inc.

Published in Canada by General Publishing Company, Ltd., 30 Lesmill Road, Don Mills, Toronto, Ontario.

Published in the United Kingdom by Constable and Company, Ltd., 3 The Lanchesters, 162–164 Fulham Palace Road, London W6 9ER.

Favorite Poems of Childhood is a new anthology of previously published children's verse, first published by Dover Publications, Inc., in 1992.

The poem "Barbershop" originally appeared in *Never Make Fun of a Turtle, My Son,* © 1969 by Martin Gardner. Reprinted courtesy of Martin Gardner.

Manufactured in the United States of America
Dover Publications, Inc., 31 East 2nd Street, Mineola, N.Y. 11501

Library of Congress Cataloging-in-Publication Data

Favorite poems of childhood / edited by Philip Smith ; illustrated by Harriet Golden.
　　　　p.　　cm. — (Dover children's thrift classics)
　　Includes indexes.
　　Summary: A collection of familiar poems for and about children, by such authors as Robert Louis Stevenson, Christina Rossetti, Eugene Field, and Sarah Josepha Hale.
　　ISBN 0-486-27089-0 (pbk.)
　　1. Children's poetry, English. 2. Children's poetry, American. [1. English poetry—Collections. 2. American poetry—Collections.]
I. Smith, Philip, 1967–　　II. Golden, Harriet, ill. III. Series.
PR1175.3.F38　1992
821.008'09282—dc20　　　　　　　　　　　　　　　　　92-21799
　　　　　　　　　　　　　　　　　　　　　　　　　　　　　　　CIP
　　　　　　　　　　　　　　　　　　　　　　　　　　　　　　　AC

Note

THIS VOLUME contains a sampling of the most familiar and acclaimed poems written for and about the very young. These verses will appeal to both young and old alike, and represent the talents of many authors famous for adult- as well as child-oriented works. The many different poem forms displayed here suggest just a few of the countless possibilities afforded by imaginative use of rhyme, rhythm, line length and treatment of subject matter. After you read these poems you may use your imagination to create original works of your own.

Contents

Contents

List of Illustrations

The Land of Nod

From breakfast on through all the day
At home among my friends I stay,
But every night I go abroad
Afar into the land of Nod.

All by myself I have to go,
With none to tell me what to do—
All alone beside the streams
And up the mountain-sides of dreams.

The strangest things are there for me,
Both things to eat and things to see,
And many frightening sights abroad
Till morning in the land of Nod.

Try as I like to find the way,
I never can get back by day,
Nor can remember plain and clear
The curious music that I hear.

—ROBERT LOUIS STEVENSON

1

Hurt No Living Thing

Hurt no living thing:
  Ladybird, nor butterfly,
Nor moth with dusty wing,
  Nor cricket chirping cheerily,
Nor grasshopper so light of leap,
  Nor dancing gnat, nor beetle fat,
Nor harmless worms that creep.

—CHRISTINA ROSSETTI

The Cat of Cats

I am the cat of cats. I am
The everlasting cat!
Cunning, and old, and sleek as jam,
The everlasting cat!
I hunt the vermin in the night—
The everlasting cat!
For I see best without the light—
The everlasting cat!

—WILLIAM BRIGHTY RANDS

I Love Little Pussy

I love little Pussy.
   Her coat is so warm,
And if I don't hurt her,
   She'll do me no harm.
So I'll not pull her tail,
   Or drive her away,
But Pussy and I
   Very gently will play,
She will sit by my side,
   And I'll give her her food,
And she'll like me because
   I am gentle and good.

I'll pat little Pussy,
   And then she will purr,
And thus show her thanks
   For my kindness to her;
I'll not pinch her ears,
   Nor tread on her paws,
Lest I should provoke her
   To use her sharp claws;
I never will vex her,
   Nor make her displeased,
For Pussy can't bear
   To be worried or teased.

—JANE TAYLOR

Mary's Lamb

Mary had a little lamb,
    Its fleece was white as snow;
And everywhere that Mary went,
    The lamb was sure to go.

He followed her to school one day,
    Which was against the rule;
It made the children laugh and play
    To see a lamb at school.

And so the teacher turned him out,
    But still he lingered near,
And waited patiently about
    Till Mary did appear.

Then he ran to her, and laid
    His head upon her arm,
As if he said, "I'm not afraid—
    You'll keep me from all harm."

"What makes the lamb love Mary so?"
    The eager children cried.
"Oh, Mary loves the lamb, you know,"
    The teacher quick replied.

And you each gentle animal
    In confidence may bind,
And make them follow at your will,
    If you are only kind.

—SARAH JOSEPHA HALE

He followed her to school one day.

Holding Hands

Elephants walking
Along the trails

Are holding hands
By holding tails.

Trunks and tails
Are handy things

When elephants walk
In Circus rings.

Elephants work
And elephants play

And elephants walk
And feel so gay.

And when they walk—
It never fails

They're holding hands
By holding tails.

—LENORE M. LINK

The Field Mouse

When the moon shines o'er the corn
and the beetle drones his horn,
And the flittermice swift fly,
And the nightjars swooping cry,
And the young hares run and leap,
We waken from our sleep.

And we climb with tiny feet
And we munch the green corn sweet
With startled eyes for fear
The white owl should fly near,
Or long slim weasel spring
Upon us where we swing.

We do not hurt at all;
Is there not room for all
Within the happy world?
All day we lie close curled
In drowsy sleep, nor rise
Till through the dusky skies
The moon shines o'er the corn
And the beetle drones his horn.

—WILLIAM SHARP

Mr. Finney's Turnip

Mr. Finney had a turnip
  And it grew and it grew;
And it grew behind the barn,
  And that turnip did no harm.

There it grew and it grew
  Till it could grow no longer;
Then his daughter Lizzie picked it
  And put it in the cellar.

There it lay and it lay
  Till it began to rot;
And his daughter Susie took it
  And put it in the pot.

And they boiled it and boiled it
  As long as they were able,
And then his daughters took it
  And put it on the table.

Mr. Finney and his wife
  They sat down to sup;
And they ate and they ate
  And they ate that turnip up.

—Anonymous

What Do We Plant?

What do we plant when we plant the tree?
We plant the ship which will cross the sea.
We plant the mast to carry the sails;
We plant the planks to withstand the gales—
The keel, the keelson, the beam, the knee;
We plant the ship when we plant the tree.

What do we plant when we plant the tree?
We plant the houses for you and me.
We plant the rafters, the shingles, the floors,
We plant the studding, the lath, the doors,
The beams and siding, all parts that be;
We plant the house when we plant the tree.

What do we plant when we plant the tree?
A thousand things that we daily see;
We plant the spire that out-towers the crag,
We plant the staff for our country's flag,
We plant the shade, from the hot sun free;
We plant all these when we plant the tree.

—HENRY ABBEY

A Wee Little Worm

A wee little worm in a hickory-nut
   Sang, happy as he could be,
"O I live in the heart of the whole round world,
   And it all belongs to me!"

—JAMES WHITCOMB RILEY

Trees

(FOR MRS. HENRY MILLS ALDEN)

I think that I shall never see
A poem lovely as a tree.

A tree whose hungry mouth is prest
Against the earth's sweet flowing breast;

A tree that looks at God all day,
And lifts her leafy arms to pray;

A tree that may in Summer wear
A nest of robins in her hair;

Upon whose bosom snow has lain;
Who intimately lives with rain.

Poems are made by fools like me,
But only God can make a tree.

—JOYCE KILMER

Trees

The Oak is called the king of trees,
The Aspen quivers in the breeze,
The Poplar grows up straight and tall,
The Peach tree spreads along the wall,
The Sycamore gives pleasant shade,
The Willow droops in watery glade,
The Fir tree useful timber gives,
The Beech amid the forest lives.

—SARA COLERIDGE

A Frisky Lamb

A frisky lamb
And a frisky child
Playing their pranks
    In a cowslip meadow:
The sky all blue
And the air all mild
And the fields all sun
    And the lanes half shadow.

—CHRISTINA ROSSETTI

Whisky Frisky

Whisky, frisky,
Hipperty hop,
Up he goes
To the tree top!

Whirly, twirly,
Round and round,
Down he scampers
To the ground.

Furly, curly,
What a tail,
Tall as a feather,
Broad as a sail.

Where's his supper?
In the shell.
Snappy, cracky,
Out it fell.

—ANONYMOUS

Nurse's Song

When the voices of children are heard on the
    green,
And laughing is heard on the hill,
My heart is at rest within my breast,
And everything else is still.

"Then come home, my children, the sun is gone
    down.
And the dews of night arise;
Come, come, leave off play, and let us away
Till the morning appears in the skies."

"No, no, let us play, for it is yet day,
And we cannot go to sleep;
Besides, in the sky the little birds fly,
And the hills are all cover'd with sheep."

"Well, well, go & play till the light fades away,
And then go home to bed."
The little ones leaped & shouted & laugh'd
And all the hills ecchoed.

—WILLIAM BLAKE

The Three Little Kittens

Three little kittens lost their mittens;
  And they began to cry,
    "Oh, mother dear,
    We very much fear
That we have lost our mittens."
    "Lost your mittens!
    You naughty kittens!
Then you shall have no pie!"
      "Mee-ow, mee-ow, mee-ow."
"No, you shall have no pie."
      "Mee-ow, mee-ow, mee-ow."

The three little kittens found their mittens;
  And they began to cry,
    "Oh, mother dear,
    See here, see here!
See, we have found our mittens!"
    "Put on your mittens,
    You silly kittens,
And you may have some pie."
      "Purr-r, purr-r, purr-r,
Oh, let us have the pie!
      Purr-r, purr-r, purr-r."

The three little kittens put on their mittens,
  And soon ate up the pie;
    "Oh, mother dear,
    We greatly fear
That we have soiled our mittens!"

"Soiled your mittens!
    You naughty kittens!"
Then they began to sigh,
        "Mee-ow, mee-ow, mee-ow."
Then they began to sigh,
        "Mee-ow, mee-ow, mee-ow."

The three little kittens washed their mittens,
    And hung them out to dry;
        "Oh, mother dear,
        Do not you hear
That we have washed our mittens?"
    "Washed your mittens!
    Oh, you're good kittens!
But I smell a rat close by,
        Hush, hush! Mee-ow, mee-ow."
"We smell a rat close by,
        Mee-ow, mee-ow, mee-ow."

                        —Eliza Lee Follen

There Were Two Ghostesses

There were two ghostesses,
Sitting on two postesses,
Eating bread and toastesses.
Weren't they beastesses
To make such feastesses?

                        —Anonymous

Jabberwocky

'Twas brillig, and the slithy toves
  Did gyre and gimble in the wabe;
All mimsy were the borogoves,
    And the mome raths outgrabe.

"Beware the Jabberwock, my son!
  The jaws that bite, the claws that catch!
Beware the Jubjub bird, and shun
    The frumious Bandersnatch!"

He took his vorpal sword in hand:
  Long time the manxome foe he sought—
So rested he by the Tumtum tree,
    And stood awhile in thought.

And as in uffish thought he stood,
  The Jabberwock, with eyes of flame,
Came whiffling through the tulgey wood,
    And burbled as it came!

One, two! One, two! And through and through
  The vorpal blade went snicker-snack!
He left it dead, and with its head
    He went galumphing back.

"And hast thou slain the Jabberwock?
  Come to my arms, my beamish boy!
O frabjous day! Callooh! Callay!"
    He chortled in his joy.

'Twas brillig, and the slithy toves
  Did gyre and gimble in the wabe;
All mimsy were the borogoves,
  And the mome raths outgrabe.

—LEWIS CARROLL

Only One Mother

Hundreds of stars in the pretty sky,
  Hundreds of shells on the shore together,
Hundreds of birds that go singing by,
  Hundreds of lambs in the sunny weather.

Hundreds of dewdrops to greet the dawn,
  Hundreds of bees in the purple clover,
Hundreds of butterflies on the lawn,
  But only one mother the wide world over.

—GEORGE COOPER

The Cow

The friendly cow all red and white,
    I love with all my heart:
She gives me cream with all her might,
    To eat with apple-tart.

She wanders lowing here and there,
    And yet she cannot stray,
All in the pleasant open air,
    The pleasant light of day;

And blown by all the winds that pass
    And wet with all the showers,
She walks among the meadow grass
    And eats the meadow flowers.

—ROBERT LOUIS STEVENSON

Tomorrow's the Fair

Tomorrow's the fair,
And I shall be there,
Stuffing my guts
With gingerbread nuts.

—ANONYMOUS

The Duel

The gingham dog and the calico cat
Side by side on the table sat;
'T was half-past twelve, and (what do you
    think!)
Nor one nor t' other had slept a wink!
  The old Dutch clock and the Chinese plate
  Appeared to know as sure as fate
There was going to be a terrible spat.
    (I was n't there; I simply state
    What was told to me by the Chinese
      plate!)

The gingham dog went "Bow-wow-wow!"
And the calico cat replied "Mee-ow!"
The air was littered, an hour or so,
With bits of gingham and calico,
  While the old Dutch clock in the chimney-
    place
  Up with its hands before its face,
For it always dreaded a family row!
    (Now mind: I'm only telling you
    What the old Dutch clock declares is
      true!)

The Chinese plate looked very blue,
And wailed, "Oh, dear! what shall we do!"
But the gingham dog and the calico cat
Wallowed this way and tumbled that,

There was going to be a terrible spat.

Employing every tooth and claw
In the awfullest way you ever saw—
And, oh! how the gingham and calico flew!
(Don't fancy I exaggerate—
I got my news from the Chinese plate!)

Next morning, where the two had sat
They found no trace of dog or cat;
And some folks think unto this day
That burglars stole that pair away!
But the truth about the cat and pup
Is this: they ate each other up!
Now what do you really think of that!
(The old Dutch clock it told me so,
And that is how I came to know.)

—EUGENE FIELD

The Moon's the North Wind's Cooky

(WHAT THE LITTLE GIRL SAID)

The Moon's the North Wind's cooky.
He bites it, day by day,
Until there's but a rim of scraps
That crumble all away.

The South Wind is a baker.
He kneads clouds in his den,
And bakes a crisp new moon *that . . .*
greedy
North . . . Wind . . . eats . . . again!

—VACHEL LINDSAY

Mr. Moon

A SONG OF THE LITTLE PEOPLE

O Moon, Mr. Moon,
When you comin' down?
Down on the hilltop,
Down in the glen,
Out in the clearin',
To play with little men?
Moon, Mr. Moon,
When you comin' down?

. . . . . .

O Mr. Moon,
Hurry up along!
The reeds in the current
Are whisperin' slow;
The river's a-wimplin'
To and fro.
Hurry up along,
Or you'll miss the song!
Moon, Mr. Moon,
When you comin' down?

. . . . . .

O Moon, Mr. Moon,
When you comin' down?

Down where the Good Folk
Dance in a ring,
Down where the Little Folk
Sing?
Moon, Mr. Moon,
When you comin' down?

—BLISS CARMAN

Judging by Appearances

An old Jack-o'-lantern lay on the ground;
He looked at the Moon-man, yellow and round.

The old Jack-o'-lantern gazed and he gazed,
And still as he looked he grew more amazed.

Then said Jack-o'-lantern, "How can it be
That fellow up there looks so much like me?

"I s'pose he must be a brother of mine,
And somebody cut *him*, *too*, from the vine.

"He looks very grand up there in the sky;
But I know just how 'twill be, by and by.

"He's proud of his shining, I have no doubt,
But just wait until *his* candle goes out!"

—EMILIE POULSSON

The Dinkey-Bird

In an ocean, 'way out yonder
   (As all sapient people know),
Is the land of Wonder-Wander,
   Whither children love to go;
It's their playing, romping, swinging,
   That give great joy to me
While the Dinkey-Bird goes singing
   In the amfalula tree!

There the gum-drops grow like cherries,
   And taffy's thick as peas—
Caramels you pick like berries
   When, and where, and how you please;
Big red sugar-plums are clinging
   To the cliffs beside that sea
Where the Dinkey-Bird is singing
   In the amfalula tree.

So when children shout and scamper
   And make merry all the day,
When there's naught to put a damper
   To the ardor of their play;
When I hear their laughter ringing,
   Then I'm sure as sure can be
That the Dinkey-Bird is singing
   In the amfalula tree.

For the Dinkey-Bird's bravuras
    And staccatos are so sweet—
His roulades, appoggiaturas,
    And robustos so complete,
That the youth of every nation—
    Be they near or far away—
Have especial delectation
    In that gladsome roundelay.

Their eyes grow bright and brighter,
    Their lungs begin to crow,
Their hearts get light and lighter,
    And their cheeks are all aglow;
For an echo cometh bringing
    The news to all and me,
That the Dinkey-Bird is singing
    In the amfalula tree.

I'm sure you like to go there
    To see your feathered friend—
And so many goodies grow there
    You would like to comprehend!
Speed, little dreams, your winging
    To that land across the sea,
Where the Dinkey-Bird is singing
    In the amfalula tree!

                    —EUGENE FIELD

The Elf and the Dormouse

Under a toadstool
   Crept a wee Elf,
Out of the rain
   To shelter himself.

Under the toadstool,
   Sound asleep,
Sat a big Dormouse,
   All in a heap.

Trembled the wee Elf,
   Frightened, and yet
Fearing to fly away
   Lest he get wet.

To the next shelter—
   Maybe a mile!
Sudden the wee Elf
   Smiled a wee smile,

Tugged till the toadstool
   Toppled in two.
Holding it over him
   Gaily he flew.

Soon he was safe home
   Dry as could be.
Soon woke the Dormouse—
   "Good gracious me!

Where is my toadstool?"
   Loud he lamented.
—And that's how umbrellas,
   First were invented.

               —OLIVER HERFORD

The Little Elf

I met a little Elfman once,
   Down where the lilies blow.
I asked him why he was so small,
   And why he didn't grow.

He slightly frowned, and with his eye
   He looked me through and through—
"I'm quite as big for me," said he,
   "As you are big for you!"

            —JOHN KENDRICK BANGS

The Fairies

Up the airy mountain,
    Down the rushy glen,
We daren't go a-hunting
    For fear of little men;
Wee folk, good folk,
    Trooping all together;
Green jacket, red cap,
    And white owl's feather!

Down along the rocky shore
    Some make their home,
They live on crispy pancakes
    Of yellow tide-foam;
Some in the reeds
    Of the black mountain-lake,
With frogs for their watch-dogs,
    All night awake.

High on the hill-top
    The old King sits;
He is now so old and gray
    He's nigh lost his wits.
With a bridge of white mist
    Columbkill he crosses,

Wee folk, good folk.

On his stately journeys
  From Slieveleague to Rosses;
Or going up with music
  On cold starry nights,
To sup with the Queen
  Of the gay Northern Lights.

They stole little Bridget
  For seven years long;
When she came down again
  Her friends were all gone.
They took her lightly back,
  Between the night and morrow,
They thought that she was fast asleep,
  But she was dead with sorrow.
They have kept her ever since
  Deep within the lake,
On a bed of flag-leaves,
  Watching till she wake.

By the craggy hill-side,
  Through the mosses bare,
They have planted thorn-trees
  For pleasure here and there.
Is any man so daring
  As dig them up in spite,

He shall find their sharpest thorns
 In his bed at night.

Up the airy mountain,
 Down the rushy glen,
We daren't go a-hunting
 For fear of little men;
Wee folk, good folk,
 Trooping all together;
Green jacket, red cap,
 And white owl's feather!

     —WILLIAM ALLINGHAM

An Unsuspected Fact

If down his throat a man should choose
In fun, to jump or slide,
He'd scrape his shoes against his teeth,
Nor dirt his own inside.
But if his teeth were lost and gone,
And not a stump to scrape upon,
He'd see at once how very pat
His tongue lay there by way of mat,
And he would wipe his feet on *that!*

     —EDWARD CANNON

Minnie and Winnie

Minnie and Winnie
  Slept in a shell.
Sleep, little ladies!
  And they slept well.

Pink was the shell within,
  Silver without;
Sounds of the great sea
  Wandered about.

Sleep little ladies!
  Wake not soon!
Echo on echo
  Dies to the moon.

Two bright stars
  Peep'd into the shell,
What are they dreaming of?
  Who can tell?

Started a green linnet
  Out of the croft;
Wake, little ladies,
  The sun is aloft!

—ALFRED, LORD TENNYSON

A Sea-Song from the Shore

Hail! Ho!
Sail! Ho!
Ahoy! Ahoy! Ahoy!
    Who calls to me,
    So far at sea?
Only a little boy!

Sail! Ho!
Hail! Ho!
The sailor he sails the sea;
    I wish he would capture
    A little sea-horse
And send him home to me.

I wish, as he sails
Through the tropical gales,
He would catch me a sea-bird, too,
    With its silver wings
    And the song it sings,
And its breast of down and dew!

I wish he would catch me a
Little mermaid,
Some island where he lands,
    With her dripping curls,
    And her crown of pearls,
And the looking-glass in her hands!

—JAMES WHITCOMB RILEY

Ducks' Ditty

All along the backwater,
Through the rushes tall,
Ducks are a-dabbling,
Up tails all!

Ducks' tails, drakes' tails,
Yellow feet a-quiver,
Yellow bills all out of sight
Busy in the river!

Slushy green undergrowth
Where the roach swim—
Here we keep our larder,
Cool and full and dim.

Everyone for what he likes!
We like to be
Heads down, tails up,
Dabbling free!

High in the blue above
Swifts whirl and call—
We are down a-dabbling
Up tails all!

—KENNETH GRAHAME

Swimming

When all the days are hot and long
And robin bird has ceased his song,
I go swimming every day
And have the finest kind of play.

I've learned to dive and I can float
As easily as does a boat;
I splash and plunge and laugh and shout
Till Daddy tells me to come out.

It's much too soon; I'd like to cry
For I can see the ducks go by,
And Daddy Duck—how I love him—
He lets his children swim and swim!

I feel that I would be in luck
If I could only be a duck!

—CLINTON SCOLLARD

If

If all the land were apple-pie,
And all the sea were ink;
And all the trees were bread and cheese,
What should we do for drink?

—ANONYMOUS

The Fisherman

The fisherman goes out at dawn
    When every one's abed,
And from the bottom of the sea
    Draws up his daily bread.

His life is strange; half on the shore
    And half upon the sea—
Not quite a fish, and yet not quite
    The same as you and me.

The fisherman has curious eyes;
    They make you feel so queer,
As if they had seen many things
    Of wonder and of fear.

They're like the sea on foggy days,—
    Not gray, nor yet quite blue;
They're like the wondrous tales he tells—
    Not quite—yet maybe—true.

He knows so much of boats and tides,
    Of winds and clouds and sky!
But when I tell of city things,
    He sniffs and shuts one eye!

—ABBIE FARWELL BROWN

O Sailor, Come Ashore

O sailor, come ashore,
    What have you brought for me?
Red coral, white coral,
    Coral from the sea.

I did not dig it from the ground,
    Nor pluck it from a tree;
Feeble insects made it
    In the stormy sea.

—CHRISTINA ROSSETTI

In the Night

The night was growing old
    As she trudged through snow and sleet;
Her nose was long and cold,
    And her shoes were full of feet.

—ANONYMOUS

Dutch Lullaby

Wynken, Blynken, and Nod one night
  Sailed off in a wooden shoe,—
Sailed on a river of misty light
  Into a sea of dew.
"Where are you going, and what do you wish?"
  The old moon asked the three.
"We have come to fish for the herring-fish
  That live in this beautiful sea;
  Nets of silver and gold have we,"
        Said Wynken,
        Blynken,
        And Nod.

The old moon laughed and sung a song,
  As they rocked in the wooden shoe;
And the wind that sped them all night long
  Ruffled the waves of dew;
The little stars were the herring-fish
  That lived in the beautiful sea.
"Now cast your nets wherever you wish,
  But never afeard are we!"
  So cried the stars to the fishermen three,
        Wynken,
        Blynken,
        And Nod.

All night long their nets they threw
  For the fish in the twinkling foam,

Then down from the sky came the wooden
    shoe,
  Bringing the fishermen home;
'T was all so pretty a sail, it seemed
  As if it could not be;
And some folk thought 't was a dream they'd
    dreamed
  Of sailing that beautiful sea;
  But I shall name you the fishermen three:
        Wynken,
        Blynken,
        And Nod.

Wynken and Blynken are two little eyes,
  And Nod is a little head,
And the wooden shoe that sailed the skies
  Is a wee one's trundle-bed;
So shut your eyes while Mother sings
  Of wonderful sights that be,
And you shall see the beautiful things
  As you rock on the misty sea
  Where the old shoe rocked the fishermen
    three,—
        Wynken,
        Blynken,
        And Nod.

              —EUGENE FIELD

The Walrus and the Carpenter

The sun was shining on the sea,
    Shining with all his might:
He did his very best to make
    The billows smooth and bright—
And this was odd, because it was
    The middle of the night.

The moon was shining sulkily,
    Because she thought the sun
Had got no business to be there
    After the day was done—
"It's very rude of him," she said,
    "To come and spoil the fun!"

The sea was wet as wet could be,
    The sands were dry as dry.
You could not see a cloud, because
    No cloud was in the sky:
No birds were flying overhead—
    There were no birds to fly.

The Walrus and the Carpenter
    Were walking close at hand;
They wept like anything to see
    Such quantities of sand:
"If this were only cleared away,"
    They said, "it *would* be grand!"

"If seven maids with seven mops
    Swept it for half a year,

Do you suppose," the Walrus said,
　"That they could get it clear?"
"I doubt it," said the Carpenter,
　And shed a bitter tear.

"O Oysters, come and walk with us!"
　The Walrus did beseech.
"A pleasant walk, a pleasant talk,
　Along the briny beach:
We cannot do with more than four,
　To give a hand to each."

The eldest Oyster looked at him,
　But never a word he said:
The eldest Oyster winked his eye,
　And shook his heavy head—
Meaning to say he did not choose
　To leave the oyster-bed.

But four young Oysters hurried up,
　All eager for the treat:
Their coats were brushed, their faces
　　washed,
　Their shoes were clean and neat—
And this was odd, because, you know,
　They hadn't any feet.

Four other Oysters followed them,
　And yet another four;
And thick and fast they came at last,
　And more, and more, and more—
All hopping through the frothy waves,
　And scrambling to the shore.

The Walrus and the Carpenter
   Walked on a mile or so,
And then they rested on a rock
   Conveniently low:
And all the little Oysters stood
   And waited in a row.

"The time has come," the Walrus said,
   "To talk of many things:
Of shoes—and ships—and sealing-wax—
   Of cabbages—and kings—
And why the sea is boiling hot—
   And whether pigs have wings."

"But, wait a bit," the Oysters cried,
   "Before we have our chat;
For some of us are out of breath,
   And all of us are fat!"
"No hurry!" said the Carpenter.
   They thanked him much for that.

"A loaf of bread," the Walrus said,
   "Is what we chiefly need:
Pepper and vinegar besides
   Are very good indeed—
Now if you're ready, Oysters dear,
   We can begin to feed."

"But not on us!" the Oysters cried,
   Turning a little blue.
"After such kindness, that would be
   A dismal thing to do!"

"The night is fine," the Walrus said.
   "Do you admire the view?

"It was so kind of you to come!
   And you are very nice!"
The Carpenter said nothing but
   "Cut me another slice:
I wish you were not quite so deaf—
   I've had to ask you twice!"

"It seems a shame," the Walrus said,
   "To play them such a trick,
After we've brought them out so far,
   And made them trot so quick!"
The Carpenter said nothing but
   "The butter's spread too thick!"

"I weep for you," the Walrus said:
   "I deeply sympathise."
With sobs and tears he sorted out
   Those of the largest size,
Holding his pocket-handkerchief
   Before his streaming eyes.

"O Oysters," said the Carpenter,
   "You've had a pleasant run!
Shall we be trotting home again?"
   But answer came there none—
And this was scarcely odd, because
   They'd eaten every one.

—LEWIS CARROLL

Laughing Song

When the green woods laugh with the voice of
 joy,
And the dimpling stream runs laughing by;
When the air does laugh with our merry wit,
And the green hill laughs with the noise of it;

When the meadows laugh with lively green,
And the grasshopper laughs in the merry scene;
When Mary, and Susan, and Emily
With their sweet round mouths sing, "Ha, ha, he!"

When the painted birds laugh in the shade,
Where our table with cherries and nuts is
 spread:
Come live, and be merry, and join with me,
To sing the sweet chorus of "Ha, ha, he!"

—WILLIAM BLAKE

The Man in the Wilderness

The man in the wilderness asked of me,
How many strawberries grow in the sea?
I answered him as I thought good,
As many red herrings as grow in the wood.

—ANONYMOUS

What Is Pink?

What is pink? a rose is pink
By the fountain's brink.
What is red? a poppy's red
In its barley bed.
What is blue? the sky is blue
Where the clouds float thro'.
What is white? a swan is white
Sailing in the light.
What is yellow? pears are yellow,
Rich and ripe and mellow.
What is green? the grass is green,
With small flowers between.
What is violet? clouds are violet
In the summer twilight.
What is orange? why, an orange,
Just an orange!

—CHRISTINA ROSSETTI

The Purple Cow

I never saw a Purple Cow,
　I never hope to see one;
But I can tell you, anyhow,
　I'd rather see than be one.

—GELETT BURGESS

The Owl and the Pussy-cat

The Owl and the Pussy-cat went to sea
    In a beautiful pea-green boat,
They took some honey, and plenty of money,
    Wrapped up in a five-pound note.
The Owl looked up to the stars above,
    And sang to a small guitar,
"O lovely Pussy! O Pussy, my love,
    What a beautiful Pussy you are,
            You are,
            You are!
    What a beautiful Pussy you are!"

II

Pussy said to the Owl, "You elegant fowl!
    How charmingly sweet you sing!
O let us be married! too long we have
        tarried:
    But what shall we do for a ring?"
They sailed away, for a year and a day,
    To the land where the Bong-tree grows
And there in a wood a Piggy-wig stood
    With a ring at the end of his nose,
            His nose,
            His nose,
    With a ring at the end of his nose.

"What a beautiful Pussy you are!"

III

"Dear Pig, are you willing to sell for one shilling
 Your ring?" Said the Piggy, "I will,"
So they took it away, and were married next day
 By the Turkey who lives on the hill.
They dined on mince, and slices of quince,
 Which they ate with a runcible spoon;
And hand in hand, on the edge of the sand,
 They danced by the light of the moon,
   The moon,
   The moon,
 They danced by the light of the moon.

—EDWARD LEAR

Antigonish

As I was going up the stair
I met a man who wasn't there;
He wasn't there again today—
I wish, I *wish*, he'd stay away.

—HUGHES MEARNS

There Was a Little Girl

There was a little girl,
And she had a little curl
   Right in the middle of her forehead.
When she was good
She was very, very good,
   And when she was bad she was horrid.

One day she went upstairs,
When her parents, unawares,
   In the kitchen were occupied with meals
And she stood upon her head
In her little trundle-bed,
   And then began hooraying with her heels.

Her mother heard the noise,
And she thought it was the boys
   A-playing at a combat in the attic;
But when she climbed the stair,
And found Jemima there,
   She took and she did spank her most
      emphatic.

—ANONYMOUS

A Magician

My brother Roger said to me,
"I am a great magician. See?
I'll make your dolls all laugh and talk,
Your Teddy bear shall dance and walk,
Your little china pug shall bark,
The creatures in your Noah's ark
Shall march in order, two by two;
And I shall do these things for you
    On the thirty-first of September.

"And you shall be a princess fair,
With trailing gown and golden hair.
The prince just now looks like the cat;
He's been bewitched—I'll change all that.
You'll find the doll's house turned into
A royal palace, when I'm through.
For I'm a great magician. See?
And all this shall be done by me
    On the thirty-first of September."

Just think how splendid it will be
When Roger does these things for me.
I didn't know he was so great,
And oh, dear! I can hardly wait
    For the thirty-first of September!

—EUNICE WARD

King Arthur

When good King Arthur ruled the land,
    He was a goodly king:
He stole three pecks of barley meal,
    To make a bag-pudding.

A bag-pudding the king did make,
    And stuffed it well with plums;
And in it put great lumps of fat,
    As big as my two thumbs.

The king and queen did eat thereof,
    And noblemen beside;
And what they could not eat that night,
    The queen next morning fried.

—Anonymous

The Young Lady of Niger

There was a young lady of Niger
Who smiled as she rode on a Tiger;
    They came back from the ride
    With the lady inside,
And the smile on the face of the Tiger.

—Anonymous

Godfrey Gordon Gustavus Gore

Godfrey Gordon Gustavus Gore—
No doubt you have heard the name before—
Was a boy who never would shut a door!

The wind might whistle, the wind might roar,
And teeth be aching and throats be sore,
But still he never would shut the door.

His father would beg, his mother implore,
"Godfrey Gordon Gustavus Gore,
We really *do* wish you would shut the door!"

Their hands they wrung, their hair they tore;
But Godfrey Gordon Gustavus Gore
Was deaf as the buoy out at the Nore.

When he walked forth the folks would roar,
"Godfrey Gordon Gustavus Gore,
Why don't you think to shut the door?"

They rigged out a Shutter with sail and oar,
And threatened to pack off Gustavus Gore
On a voyage of penance to Singapore.

But he begged for mercy, and said, "No more!
Pray do not send me to Singapore
On a Shutter, and then I will shut the door!"

"You will?" said his parents; "then keep on shore!
But mind you do! For the plague is sore
Of a fellow that never will shut the door,
Godfrey Gordon Gustavus Gore!"

—WILLIAM BRIGHTY RANDS

The Rhyme of Dorothy Rose

Dorothy Rose had a turned-up nose.
Did she worry about it, do you suppose?
Oh, no; but a plan she began to hatch,
To make the rest of her features match.

First of all, she trained her eyes,
Turning them up to the sunny skies.
Look at the mud and the dust? not she!
Nothing but sunshine would Dorothy see.

A flower that droops has begun to wilt,
So up went her chin, with a saucy tilt.
An ounce of pluck's worth a pound of sigh,
And courage comes with a head held high.

Lastly, her lips turned their corners up,
Brimming with smiles like a rosy cup.
Oh, a charming child is Dorothy Rose,—
And it all began with a turned-up nose!

—PAULINE FRANCES CAMP

My Shadow

I have a little shadow that goes in and out with
  me
And what can be the use of him is more than I
  can see.
He is very, very like me from the heels up to the
  head;
And I see him jump before me, when I jump into
  my bed.

The funniest thing about him is the way he likes
  to grow—
Not at all like proper children, which is always
  very slow;
For he sometimes shoots up taller like an india-
  rubber ball,
And he sometimes gets so little that there's
  none of him at all.

He hasn't got a notion of how children ought to
  play,
And can only make a fool of me in every sort of
  way.
He stays so close beside me, he's a coward you
  can see;
I'd think shame to stick to nursie as that
  shadow sticks to me!

One morning, very early, before the sun was up,
I rose and found the singing dew on every
    buttercup;
But my lazy little shadow, like an arrant sleepy-
    head,
Had stayed at home behind me and was fast
    asleep in bed.

            —ROBERT LOUIS STEVENSON

A Tragedy

This is the short, sweet, sorrowful tale
    Of Jessica Jenkins Jones;
She planted a packet of seeds with pride
While her dog looked on with his head
     on the side
    And thought, "She's burying bones."

When Jessica left, he dug like mad
    In search of the luscious bones,
So Jessica's garden it doesn't grow,
And Jessica's dog is cross, and so
    Is Jessica Jenkins Jones.

            —DORIS WEBB

The Pantry Ghosts

Last night I had a horrid dream—
  I cannot tell you why—
Huge pies and cakes of chocolate cream
  And doughnuts passing by.

They looked at me with wicked joy.
  I thought I heard them say,
"By night we haunt the foolish boy
  That haunts our shelf by day.

"Behind us comes a nightmare grim—
  You'd better hide your head!—
And then some Things, all pale and dim;
  So crawl down in your bed.

"We never mind a little slice,—
  A bite or two,—but when
You eat *too much*, it is n't nice,
  And we shall come again!"

—Frederic Richardson

Mr. Coggs, Watchmaker

A watch will tell the time of day,
Or tell it nearly, anyway,
Excepting when it's overwound,
Or when you drop it on the ground.

If any of our watches stop,
We haste to Mr. Coggs's shop;
For though to scold us he pretends
He's quite among our special friends.

He fits a dice box in his eye,
And takes a long and thoughtful spy,
And prods the wheels, and says: "Dear,
      dear!
More carelessness I greatly fear."

And then he lays the dice box down
And frowns a most prodigious frown;
But if we ask him what's the time,
He'll make his gold repeater chime.

—EDWARD VERRALL LUCAS

Little Boy Blue

The little toy dog is covered with dust,
    But sturdy and stanch he stands;
And the little toy soldier is red with rust,
    And his musket molds in his hands.
Time was when the little toy dog was new
    And the soldier was passing fair,
And that was the time when our Little Boy
    Blue
    Kissed them and put them there.

"Now, don't you go till I come," he said,
    "And don't you make any noise!"
So toddling off to his trundle-bed
    He dreamed of the pretty toys.
And as he was dreaming, an angel song
    Awakened our Little Boy Blue,—
Oh, the years are many, the years are long,
    But the little toy friends are true.

Ay, faithful to Little Boy Blue they stand,
    Each in the same old place,
Awaiting the touch of a little hand,
    The smile of a little face.
And they wonder, as waiting these long years
    through,
    In the dust of that little chair,
What has become of our Little Boy Blue
    Since he kissed them and put them there.

                    —Eugene Field

The Quangle Wangle's Hat

I

On the top of the Crumpetty Tree
   The Quangle Wangle sat,
But his face you could not see,
   On account of his Beaver Hat.
For his Hat was a hundred and two feet wide,
With ribbons and bibbons on every side
And bells, and buttons, and loops, and lace,
   So that nobody ever could see the face
      Of the Quangle Wangle Quee.

II

The Quangle Wangle said
   To himself on the Crumpetty Tree,—
"Jam; and jelly; and bread;
   "Are the best food for me!
"But the longer I live on this Crumpetty Tree
"The plainer than ever it seems to me
"That very few people come this way
"And that life on the whole is far from gay!"
      Said the Quangle Wangle Quee.

III

But there came to the Crumpetty Tree,
   Mr. and Mrs. Canary;
And they said,—"Did you ever see
   "Any spot so charmingly airy?

"May we build a nest on your lovely Hat?
"Mr. Quangle Wangle, grant us that!
"O please let us come and build a nest
"Of whatever material suits you best,
        "Mr. Quangle Wangle Quee!"

IV

And besides, to the Crumpetty Tree
    Came the Stork, the Duck, and the Owl;
The Snail, and the Bumble-Bee,
    The Frog, and the Fimble Fowl;
(The Fimble Fowl, with a Corkscrew leg;)
And all of them said,—"We humbly beg,
    "We may build our homes on your lovely Hat,—
"Mr. Quangle Wangle, grant us that!
        "Mr. Quangle Wangle Quee!"

V

And the Golden Grouse came there,
    And the Pobble who has no toes,—
And the small Olympian bear,—
    And the Dong with a luminous nose.
And the Blue Baboon, who played the flute,—
And the Orient Calf from the Land of Tute,—
And the Attery Squash, and the Bisky Bat,—
All came and built on the lovely Hat
        Of the Quangle Wangle Quee.

VI

And the Quangle Wangle said,
   To himself on the Crumpetty Tree,—
"When all these creatures move
   "What a wonderful noise there'll be!"
And at night by the light of the Mulberry moon
They danced to the Flute of the Blue Baboon,
On the broad green leaves of the Crumpetty
   Tree,
And all were as happy as happy could be,
     With the Quangle Wangle Quee.

—EDWARD LEAR

The Butter Betty Bought

Betty Botta bought some butter;
"But," said she, "This butter's bitter!
If I put it in my batter
It will make my batter bitter.
But a bit o' better butter
Will but make my batter better."
So she bought a bit o' butter
Better than the bitter butter,
Made her bitter batter better.
So 'twas better Betty Botta
Bought a bit o' better butter.

—ANONYMOUS

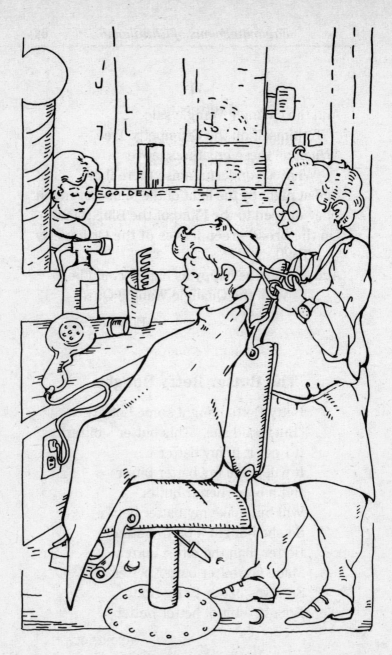

Those scissors can slip.

Barbershop

When you visit the barber
   And sit in his chair,
Don't squirm
Like a worm
   While he's cutting your hair.

Don't shiver
And quiver
   And bounce up and down.
Don't shuffle
And snuffle
   And act like a clown.

Each wiggle
Will jiggle
   The blades of the shears.
Clip-clip,
Clip-clip.
Those scissors can slip
And snip
Off a tip
   Of one of your tender pink ears!

—MARTIN GARDNER

The Raggedy Man

O The Raggedy Man! He works fer Pa;
An' he's the goodest man ever you saw!
He comes to our house every day,
An' waters the horses, an' feeds 'em hay;
An' he opens the shed—an' we all ist laugh
When he drives out our little, old, wobble-ly calf;
An' nen—ef our hired girl says he can—
He milks the cow fer 'Lizabuth Ann—
    Ain't he a' awful good Raggedy Man?
      Raggedy! Raggedy! Raggedy Man!

W'y, The Raggedy Man—he's ist so good
He splits the kindlin' an' chops the wood;
An' nen he spades in our garden, too,
An' does most things 'at *boys* can't do—
He clumbed clean up in our big tree
An' shooked a' apple down fer me—
An' 'nother 'n', too, fer 'Lizabuth Ann—
An' 'nother 'n', too, fer The Raggedy Man—
    Ain't he a' awful kind Raggedy Man?
      Raggedy! Raggedy! Raggedy Man!

An' The Raggedy Man, he knows most rhymes
An' tells 'em, if I be good, sometimes:
Knows 'bout Giunts, an' Griffuns, an' Elves,
An' the Squidgicum Squees 'at swallers
      therselves!
An' wite by the pump in our pasture-lot,
He showed me the hole 'at the Wunks is got,

'At lives 'way deep in the ground, 'an can
Turn into me, er 'Lizabuth Ann!
Er Ma, er Pa, er The Raggedy Man!
    Ain't he a funny old Raggedy Man?
        Raggedy! Raggedy! Raggedy Man!

The Raggedy Man—one time when he
Wuz makin' a little bow-'n'-orry fer me,
Says, "When *you're* big like your Pa is,
Air you go' to keep a fine store like his—
An' be a rich merchunt—an' wear fine clothes?—
Er what *air* you go' to be, goodness knows!"
An' nen he laughed at 'Lizabuth Ann,
An' I says "'M go' to be a Raggedy Man!—
    I'm ist go' to be a nice Raggedy Man!"
        Raggedy! Raggedy! Raggedy Man!

           — JAMES WHITCOMB RILEY

Great Fleas Have Little Fleas

Great fleas have little fleas upon their backs to
    bite 'em,
And little fleas have lesser fleas, and so ad
    infinitum.
And the great fleas themselves in turn have
    greater fleas to go on
While these again have greater still, and greater
    still, and so on.

           —A. DE MORGAN

The Peppery Man

The Peppery Man was cross and thin;
He scolded out and scolded in;
He shook his fist, his hair he tore;
He stamped his feet and slammed the door.

> Heigh ho, the Peppery Man,
> The rabid, crabbed Peppery Man!
> Oh, never since the world began
> Was any one like the Peppery Man.

His ugly temper was so sour
He often scolded for an hour;
He gnashed his teeth and stormed and scowled,
He snapped and snarled and yelled and howled.

He wore a fierce and savage frown;
He scolded up and scolded down;
He scolded over field and glen,
And then he scolded back again.

His neighbors, when they heard his roars,
Closed their blinds and locked their doors,
Shut their windows, sought their beds,
Stopped their ears and covered their heads.

He fretted, chafed, and boiled and fumed;
With fiery rage he was consumed,
And no one knew, when he was vexed,
What in the world would happen next.

Heigh ho, the Peppery Man,
The rabid, crabbed Peppery Man!
Oh, never since the world began
Was any one like the Peppery Man.

—ARTHUR MACY

August

Buttercup nodded and said good-by,
    Clover and daisy went off together,
But the fragrant water lilies lie
    Yet moored in the golden August weather.

The swallows chatter about their flight,
    The cricket chirps like a rare good fellow,
The asters twinkle in clusters bright,
    While the corn grows ripe and the apples
        mellow.

—CELIA THAXTER

The Mayor of Scuttleton

The Mayor of Scuttleton burned his nose
Trying to warm his copper toes;
He lost his money and spoiled his will
By signing his name with an icicle quill;
He went bareheaded, and held his breath,
And frightened his grandame most to death;
He loaded a shovel and tried to shoot,
And killed the calf in the leg of his boot;
He melted a snowbird and formed the habit
Of dancing jigs with a sad Welsh rabbit;
He lived on taffy and taxed the town;
And read his newspaper upside down;
Then he sighed and hung his hat on a feather,
And bade the townspeople come together;
But the worst of it all was, nobody knew
What the Mayor of Scuttleton next would do.

— MARY MAPES DODGE

Aunt Eliza

In the drinking-well
    (Which the plumber built her)
Aunt Eliza fell,—
    We must buy a filter.

— HARRY GRAHAM

Armies in the Fire

The lamps now glitter down the street;
Faintly sound the falling feet;
And the blue even slowly falls
About the garden trees and walls.

Now in the falling of the gloom
The red fire paints the empty room:
And warmly on the roof it looks,
And flickers on the backs of books.

Armies march by tower and spire
Of cities blazing, in the fire;—
Till as I gaze with staring eyes,
The armies fade, the lustre dies.

Then once again the glow returns;
Again the phantom city burns;
And down the red-hot valley, lo!
The phantom armies marching go!

Blinking embers, tell me true
Where are those armies marching to,
And what the burning city is
That crumbles in your furnaces!

               —ROBERT LOUIS STEVENSON

The Star

Twinkle, twinkle, little star,
How I wonder what you are!
Up above the world so high,
Like a diamond in the sky.

When the blazing sun is gone,
When he nothing shines upon,
Then you show your little light,
Twinkle, twinkle, all the night.

Then the traveller in the dark,
Thanks you for your tiny spark,
He could not see which way to go,
If you did not twinkle so.

In the dark blue sky you keep,
And often through my curtains peep,
For you never shut your eye,
Till the sun is in the sky.

As your bright and tiny spark,
Lights the traveller in the dark—
Though I know not what you are,
Twinkle, twinkle, little star.

—JANE TAYLOR

The Tyger

Tyger! Tyger! burning bright
In the forests of the night,
What immortal hand or eye
Could frame thy fearful symmetry?

In what distant deeps or skies
Burnt the fire of thine eyes?
On what wings dare he aspire?
What the hand dare sieze the fire?

And what shoulder, & what art,
Could twist the sinews of thy heart?
And when thy heart began to beat,
What dread hand? & what dread feet?

What the hammer? what the chain?
In what furnace was thy brain?
What the anvil? what dread grasp
Dare its deadly terrors clasp?

When the stars threw down their spears,
And water'd heaven with their tears,
Did he smile his work to see?
Did he who made the Lamb make thee?

Tyger! Tyger! burning bright
In the forests of the night,
What immortal hand or eye
Dare frame thy fearful symmetry?

—WILLIAM BLAKE

The Children's Hour

Between the dark and the daylight,
    When the night is beginning to lower,
Comes a pause in the day's occupations,
    That is known as the Children's Hour.

I hear in the chamber above me
    The patter of little feet,
The sounds of a door that is opened,
    And voices soft and sweet.

From my study I see in the lamplight,
    Descending the broad hall stair,
Grave Alice, and laughing Allegra,
    And Edith with golden hair.

A whisper, and then a silence:
    Yet I know by their merry eyes
They are plotting and planning together
    To take me by surprise.

A sudden rush from the stairway,
    A sudden raid from the hall!
By three doors left unguarded
    They enter my castle wall!

They climb up into my turret
    O'er the arms and back of my chair;
If I try to escape, they surround me;
    They seem to be everywhere.

They almost devour me with kisses,
    Their arms about me entwine,
Till I think of the Bishop of Bingen
    In his Mouse-Tower on the Rhine!

Do you think, O blue-eyed banditti,
    Because you have scaled the wall,
Such an old mustache as I am
    Is not a match for you all!

I have you fast in my fortress,
    And will not let you depart,
But put you down into the dungeon
    In the round-tower of my heart.

And there will I keep you forever,
    Yes, forever and a day,
Till the walls shall crumble to ruin,
    And moulder in dust away!

                —HENRY WADSWORTH LONGFELLOW

Tender-Heartedness

Little Willie, in the best of sashes,
Fell in the fire and was burned to ashes.
By and by the room grew chilly,
But no one liked to poke up Willie.

                —HARRY GRAHAM

Windy Nights

Whenever the moon and stars are set,
   Whenever the wind is high,
All night long in the dark and wet,
   A man goes riding by.
Late in the night when the fires are out,
Why does he gallop and gallop about?

Whenever the trees are crying aloud,
   And ships are tossed at sea,
By, on the highway, low and loud,
   By at the gallop goes he.
By at the gallop he goes, and then
By he comes back at the gallop again.

       —ROBERT LOUIS STEVENSON

October

October turned my maple's leaves to gold;
   The most are gone now; here and there one
      lingers.
Soon these will slip from out the twig's weak
      hold,
   Like coins between a dying miser's fingers.

       —THOMAS BAILEY ALDRICH

The Whango Tree

The woggly bird sat on the whango tree,
    Nooping the rinkum corn,
And graper and graper, alas! grew he,
    And cursed the day he was born.
His crute was clum and his voice was rum,
    As curiously thus sang he,
"Oh, would I'd been rammed and eternally clammed
    Ere I perched on this whango tree."

Now the whango tree had a bubbly thorn,
    As sharp as a nootie's bill,
And it stuck in the woggly bird's umptum lorn
    And weepadge, the smart did thrill.
He fumbled and cursed, but that wasn't the worst,
    For he couldn't at all get free,
And he cried, "I am gammed, and injustibly nammed
    On the luggardly whango tree."

And there he sits still, with no worm in his bill,
    Nor no guggledom in his nest;
He is hungry and bare, and gobliddered with care,
    And his grabbles give him no rest;
He is weary and sore and his tugmut is soar,
    And nothing to nob has he,
As he chirps, "I am blammed and corruptibly jammed,
    In this cuggerdom whango tree."

— ANONYMOUS

Little Orphant Annie

Little Orphant Annie's come to our house to stay,
An' wash the cups and saucers up, an' brush the crumbs
    away,
An' shoo the chickens off the porch, an' dust the hearth,
    an' sweep,
An' make the fire, an' bake the bread, an' earn her board-
    an'-keep;
An' all us other children, when the supper things is
    done,
We set around the kitchen fire an' has the mostest fun
A-list'nin' to the witch tales 'at Annie tells about,
An' the Gobble-uns 'at gits you
                    Ef you
                    Don't
                    Watch
                    Out!

Onc't they was a little boy wouldn't say his prayers,—
So when he went to bed at night, away upstairs,
His Mammy heerd him holler, an' his Daddy heerd him
    bawl,
An' when they turn't the kivvers down, he wasn't there
    at all!
An' they seeked him in the rafter room, an' cubbyhole,
    an' press,
An' seeked him up the chimbly flue, an' ever'wheres, I
    guess;
But all they ever found was thist his pants an' round-
    about:—

An' the Gobble-uns 'll git you

Ef you

Don't

Watch

Out!

An' one time a little girl 'ud allus laugh an' grin,
An' make fun of ever'one, an' all her blood an' kin;
An' onc't, when they was "company," an' ole folks
    was there,
She mocked 'em an' shocked 'em, an' said she didn't
    care!
An' thist as she kicked her heels, an' turn't to run an'
    hide,
They was two great big Black Things a standin' by
    her side,
An' they snatched her through the ceilin' 'fore she
    knowed what she's about!
An' the Gobble-uns 'll git you

Ef you

Don't

Watch

Out!

An' little Orphant Annie says, when the blaze is blue,
An' the lamp-wick sputters, an' the wind goes *woo-oo!*
An' you hear the crickets quit, an' the moon is gray,
An' the lightnin' bugs in dew is all squenched away,—
You better mind yer parents, and yer teachers fond
    an' dear,
An' churish them 'at loves you, an' dry the orphant's
    tear,

An' he'p the pore an' needy ones 'at clusters all about,
Er the Gobble-uns 'll git you
Ef you
Don't
Watch
Out!

—James Whitcomb Riley

Thanksgiving Day

Over the river and through the wood,
To grandfather's house we go;
The horse knows the way
To carry the sleigh
Through the white and drifted snow.

Over the river and through the wood—
Oh, how the wind does blow!
It stings the toes
And bites the nose,
As over the ground we go.

Over the river and through the wood,
To have a first-rate play.
Hear the bells ring,
"Ting-a-ling-ding!"
Hurrah for Thanksgiving Day!

Over the river and through the wood
Trot fast, my dapple-gray!

Spring over the ground,
Like a hunting-hound!
For this is Thanksgiving Day.

Over the river and through the wood,
And straight through the barnyard gate.
We seem to go
Extremely slow,—
It is so hard to wait!

Over the river and through the wood—
Now grandmother's cap I spy!
Hurrah for the fun!
Is the pudding done?
Hurrah for the pumpkin-pie!

—LYDIA MARIA CHILD

Extremes

A little boy once played so loud
That the thunder, up in a thundercloud,
Said, "Since *I* can't be heard, why, then
I'll never, never thunder again!"

And a little girl once kept so still
That she heard a fly on the window sill
Whisper and say to a ladybird,—
"She's the stillest child I ever heard!"

—JAMES WHITCOMB RILEY

Till I can see so wide.

The Swing

How do you like to go up in a swing,
    Up in the air so blue?
Oh, I do think it the pleasantest thing
    Ever a child can do!

Up in the air and over the wall,
    Till I can see so wide,
Rivers and trees and cattle and all
    Over the countryside—

Till I look down on the garden green,
    Down on the roof so brown—
Up in the air I go flying again,
    Up in the air and down!

—ROBERT LOUIS STEVENSON

A Flea and a Fly in a Flue

A flea and a fly in a flue
Were imprisoned, so what could they do?
    Said the fly, "Let us flee,"
    Said the flea, "Let us fly,"
So they flew through a flaw in the flue.

—ANONYMOUS

The Eagle

He clasps the crag with crooked hands;
Close to the sun in lonely lands,
Ringed with the azure world, he stands.

The wrinkled sea beneath him crawls;
He watches from his mountain walls,
And like a thunderbolt he falls.

—ALFRED, LORD TENNYSON

Who Has Seen the Wind?

Who has seen the wind?
   Neither I nor you:
But when the leaves hang trembling
   The wind is passing thro'.

Who has seen the wind?
   Neither you nor I:
But when the trees bow down their heads
   The wind is passing by.

—CHRISTINA ROSSETTI

I'm Nobody! Who Are You?

I'm nobody! Who are you?
Are you nobody, too?
Then there's a pair of us—don't tell!
They'd banish us, you know.

How dreary to be somebody!
How public, like a frog
To tell your name the livelong day
To an admiring bog!

—EMILY DICKINSON

November Night

Listen . . .
With faint dry sound,
Like steps of passing ghosts,
The leaves, frost-crisp'd, break from the trees
And fall.

— ADELAIDE CRAPSEY

Eldorado

Gaily bedight,
A gallant knight,
In sunshine and in shadow,
Had journeyed long,
Singing a song,
In search of Eldorado.

But he grew old—
This knight so bold—
And o'er his heart a shadow
Fell as he found
No spot of ground
That looked like Eldorado.

And, as his strength
Failed him at length,
He met a pilgrim shadow—
"Shadow," said he,
"Where can it be—
This land of Eldorado?"

"Over the Mountains
Of the Moon,
Down the Valley of the Shadow,
Ride, boldly ride,"
The shade replied,—
"If you seek for Eldorado."

—EDGAR ALLAN POE

Alphabetical List of Titles

Alphabetical List of Authors

Alphabetical List of First Lines